Jim Arnosky

Rattlesnake Dance

G. P. Putnam's Sons • New York

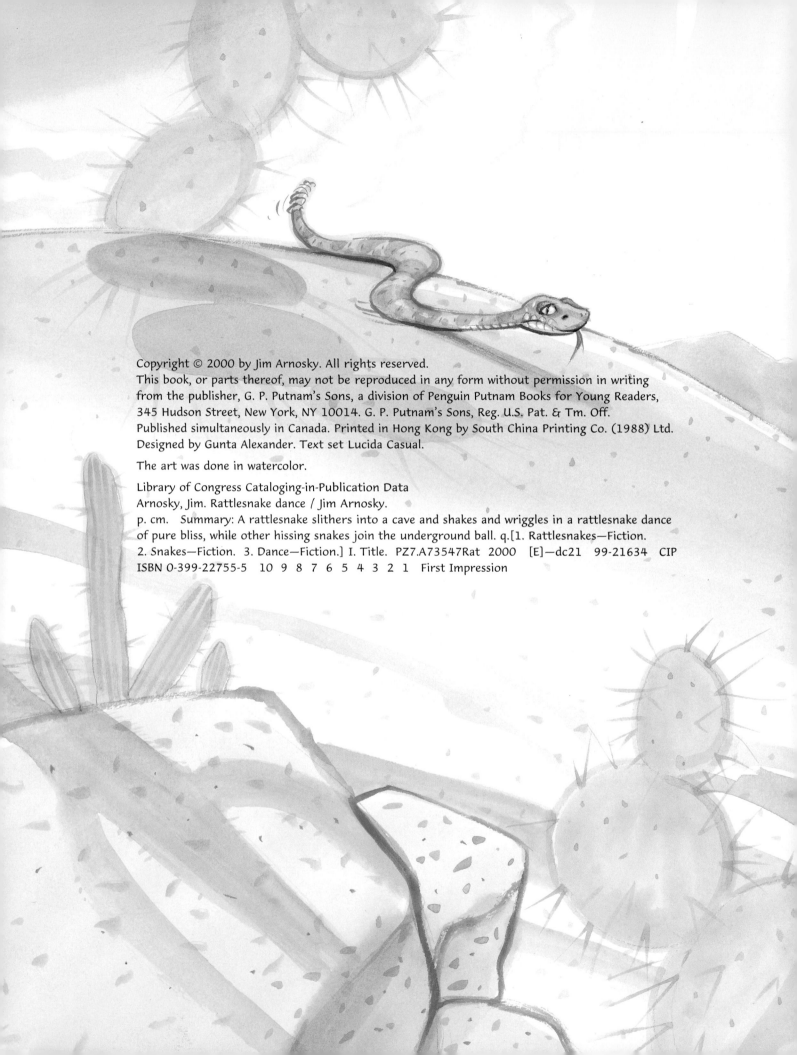

The art was done in watercolor.

Library of Congress Cataloging-in-Publication Data
Arnosky, Jim. Rattlesnake dance / Jim Arnosky.
p. cm.   Summary: A rattlesnake slithers into a cave and shakes and wriggles in a rattlesnake dance
of pure bliss, while other hissing snakes join the underground ball. q.[1. Rattlesnakes—Fiction.
2. Snakes—Fiction. 3. Dance—Fiction.] I. Title. PZ7.A73547Rat 2000   [E]—dc21   99-21634   CIP
ISBN 0-399-22755-5   10 9 8 7 6 5 4 3 2 1   First Impression

for Justin

Rattlesnake Dance

by Jim Arnosky

Musical arrangement
by Christopher Drobny
Copyright © 2000

One desert day,
hot as a frying pan,

a rattlesnake
slithered across
the sand.

He found a small hole
'neath a jagged rock.
It was shady and cool.
He was no rattlesnake fool.

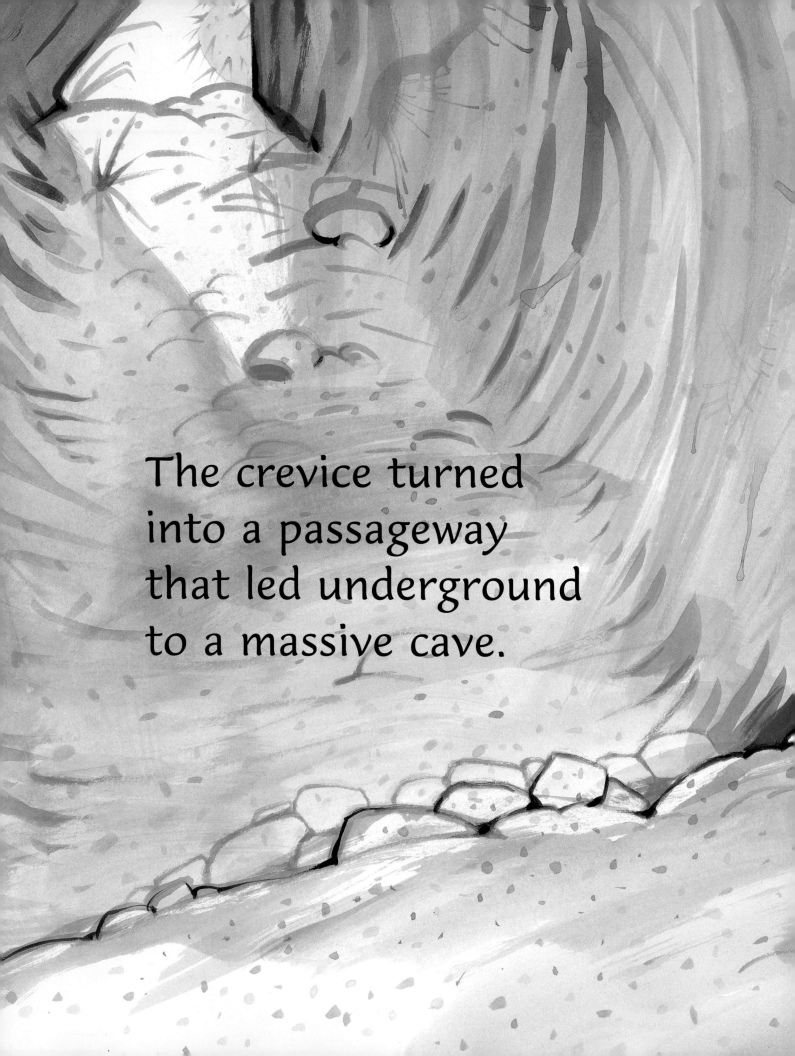

The crevice turned
into a passageway
that led underground
to a massive cave.

The snake slid along
in the darkened room.

He found a wall
and coiled in a ball.

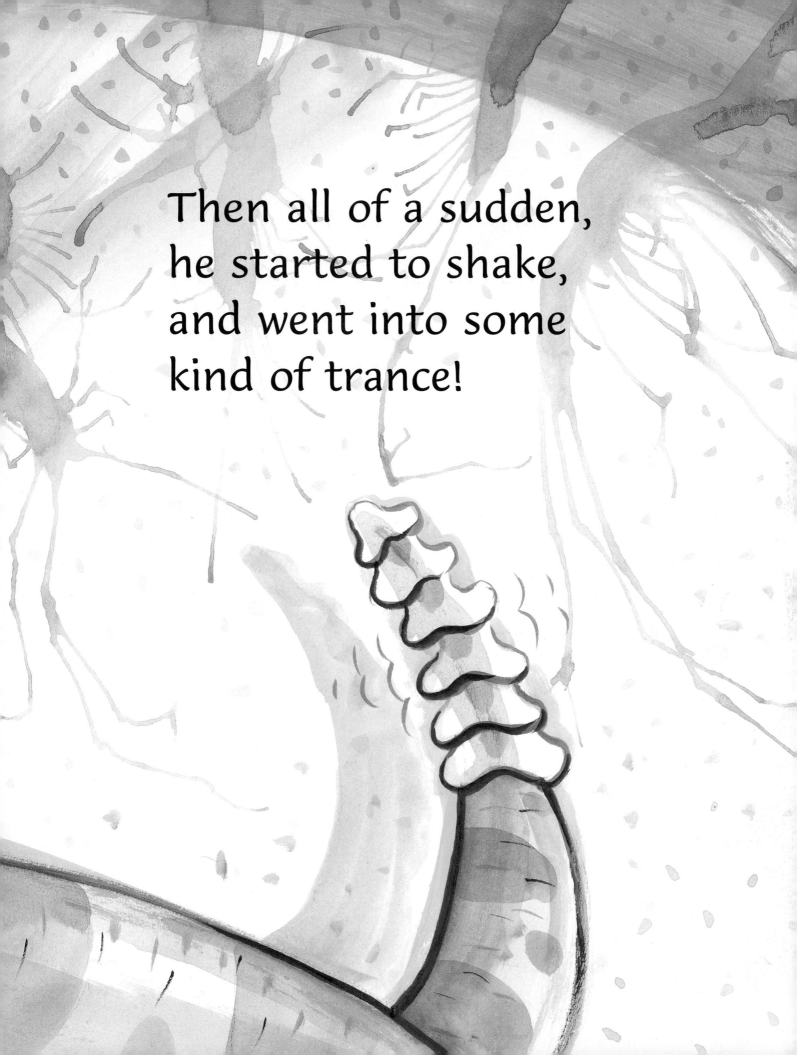

Then all of a sudden,
he started to shake,
and went into some
kind of trance!

His neck began swaying.
His rattle tail rattled.
He was doing the
Rattlesnake Dance.

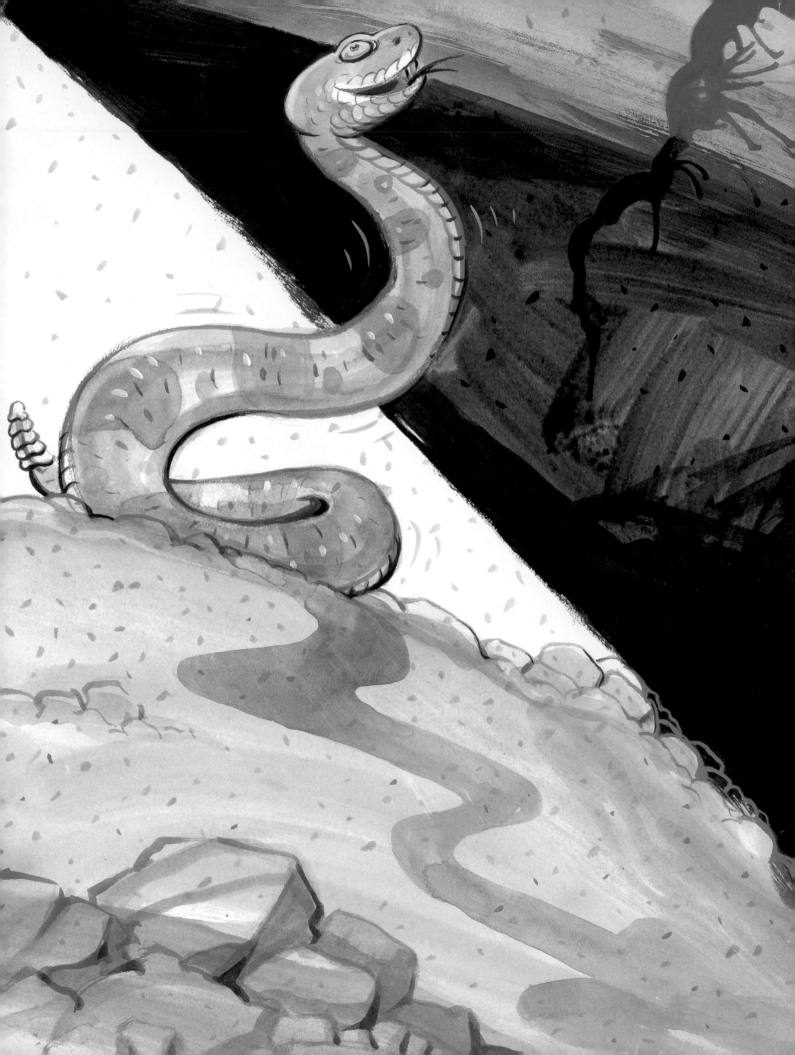

Like ghosts from the
depths of the sandy cave
came more rattlers
feeling the rhythmic wave.

Soon the place was crawling
with rattlesnakes,
all hissing away,
getting those spooky shakes.

And they wriggled and squirmed
and rattled their tails,
all glassy eyed,
deep in the trance.

They raised their heads
and swayed side to side.

They were doing the
Rattlesnake Dance.

The underground ball
lasted many days.
The snakes were caught up
in the dancing craze.

Then, one by one,
rattlers left the cave.
They had snapped out
of the trance.

It was the end
of the dance.

But they'll be back
this same time next year.
It's something they
won't want to miss.

A dance like this
is pure rattlesnake bliss!

Where they can wriggle and squirm

and sway side to side
under a powerful trance.

They slither and hiss
and rattle their tails,

all doing
the Rattlesnake Dance.

You can do
the rattlesnake
dance too!
Just hold your
arms down
at your sides
and sway
side to side
like a snake.

That's it . . .
now hiss!